Eggs i

Written by Jill Eggleton
Illustrated by Jan van der Voo

Rigby

The people in the book

Mrs. Mack

Mr. Mack

100

cosas que deberías saber sobre los

VIKINGOS

Fiona Macdonald

Asesor: Jeremy Smith

susaeta

Título original: *Vikings*

Dirección editorial: Isabel Ortiz
Traducción: Pilar Tutor
Corrección: Mª Carmen Martínez + Equipo Susaeta
Diseño: Louisa Leitao
Maquetación: Miguel Ángel San Andrés + Equipo Susaeta
Índice: Jane Parker

AGRADECIMIENTOS
Los editores desean dar las gracias a los siguientes artistas que han colaborado en el presente libro:

Peter Dennis
Mike Foster
Richard Hook
Kevin Maddison
Janos Marffy
Alessandro Menchi
Peter Sarson
Mike Saunders
Mike White
Rudi Vizi

Cómics: Mark Davis / Mackerel

Campezo, s/n-28022 Madrid
Tel.: 913 009 100-Fax: 913 009 118

The kitchen

On Saturday, Mr. and Mrs. Mack went to the store.
They got milk and bread and eggs.

Mr. Mack put the milk in the fridge.

He put the bread in the cabinet.

Mrs. Mack put the eggs in a bowl on the table.

Mr. Mack looked at the eggs on the table.
The sun was on the eggs.

"You can't put eggs in the sun," he said. **"Chickens will come out."**

Mrs. Mack laughed. **"Chickens will not come out,"** she said.

On Monday, Mr. Mack
was coming home from work.
He saw a chicken farm.
He saw...

Chickens
for sale
$3.00

Chickens
for sale
$3.00

Mr. Mack went into the farm.

"Can I have two chickens, please?" he said.

The farmer gave Mr. Mack two chickens in a box. Mr. Mack took the chickens home and...

Mr. Mack did this:

1

He took the eggs
out of the bowl.

2

He cracked
the eggs.

3

He put the eggs
in a cup.

4

He put the cup
in the fridge.

5

He put the egg
shells in the bowl.

6

He took the chickens
out of the box.

7

He put the chickens
in the bowl
with the egg shells.

Mrs. Mack will be...?

Mrs. Mack came home.
She went into the kitchen.

"Cheep, cheep, cheep,"
went the chickens in the bowl.
"Cheep, cheep, cheep."

"Look at that!" said Mrs. Mack.
"Chickens have come out of the eggs!"

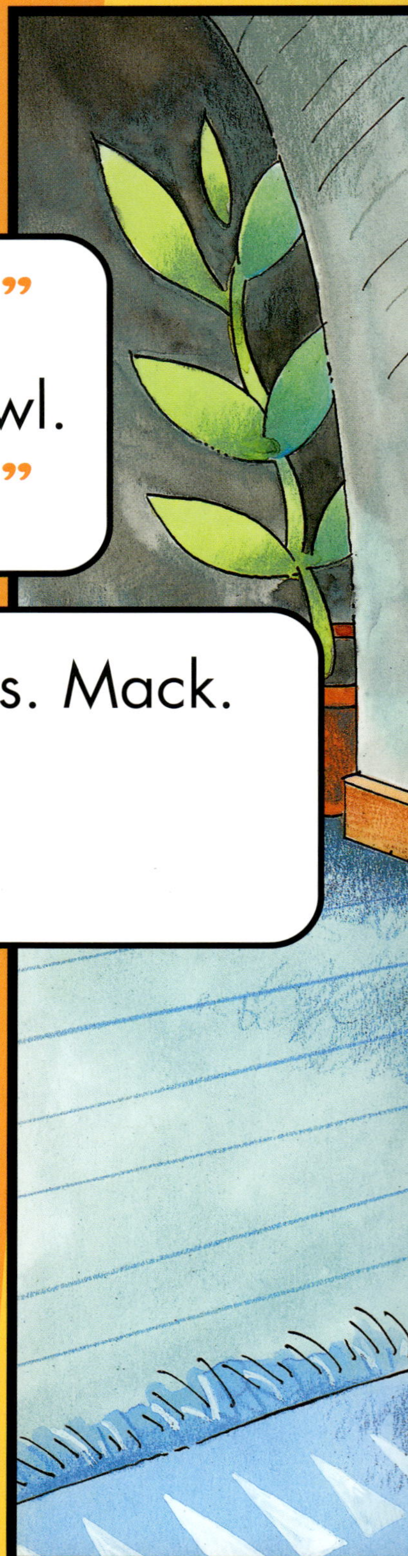

Mrs. Mack took the chickens out.
She went to see Mr. Mack.

"Look," she said.
"Chickens have come out of the eggs!"

Mrs. Mack will...

keep the chickens in the house?

make a chicken farm?

let the chickens go?

Mr. Mack looked at the chickens.

"See," he said.
"You can't put eggs in the sun.
Chickens will come out."

But Mrs. Mack said,
"Good. I'm going to put all my eggs in the sun."

Mrs. Mack looked at Mr. Mack and she laughed and laughed.

"You can go and get a BIG box of eggs!" she said.

The End

A sequence

Where do the numbers go?

5 6

4 7

3
?
?
?

Word Bank

bowl 

bread 

cabinet 

chickens 

eggs 

fridge 

gate 

milk 

shells 

table